NOTHING BUT THE TRUTH

by
Avi

Teacher Guide

Written by
Phyllis A. Green

Note

The Avon Flare paperback edition of the book was used to prepare this guide. The page references may differ in the hardcover or other paperback editions.

Please note: Please assess the appropriateness of this book for the age level and maturity of your students prior to reading and discussing it with your class.

ISBN 1-56137-740-6

Novel Units is a registered trademark of Novel Units, Inc.

Printed in the United States of America.

To order, contact your local school supply store, or—

Novel Units, Inc.
P.O. Box 791610
San Antonio, TX 78279

Web site: www.educyberstor.com

Table of Contents

Summary 3

About the Author 3

Introductory Information and Activities 4

Nineteen Chapters 12
   Chapters contain: Vocabulary Words,
   Discussion Questions and Activities,
   Predictions, Supplementary Activities

Culminating Activities 31

Vocabulary Activities 31

Assessment 35

Skills and Strategies

Comprehension
   Predicting, inference,
   comparison/contrast,
   cause-effect

Writing
   News article, letters

Vocabulary
   Prefixes/suffixes, sorting

Thinking
   Synthesis, evaluation,
   brainstorming

Listening/Speaking
   Discussion, drama

Literary Elements
   Irony, satire, story elements,
   characterization, hyperbole

Summary of *Nothing But The Truth*

A ninth-grader's suspension f singing "The Star-Spangled Banner" during homeroom becomes a national news sto   The story is revealed without a narrator, through school memos, diary entries, letter: lialogues, newspaper articles, and radio talk show scripts. The reader sees differing p s of view about the incident and is able to root out the real problems affecting the cident. The players are Philip Malloy (the ninth grader), Margaret Narwin (the hor oom teacher), the assistant principal, the principal, the superintendent of school: nd Ted Griffen (who is running for the school board).

About the Author

Avi, whose full name is i Wortis, writes under the three-letter moniker. Born in 1937, in New York City, he grew up an artistic environment. Both parents, his great-grandparents, his grandmother, a twin er, and an aunt were writers. Within the extended family were painters, a composer id others active in music, theater, and film. Raised in Brooklyn, his family was active po! ally in various liberal ideas. As a student he suffered with dysgraphia, a marginal impairmer n his writing abilities that caused him to reverse letters or misspell words.

An avid reader, he nsiders this love to have been his first step toward writing professionally. He attended Antic University (where he studied playwriting as a prelude to his writing career) and earne a B.A. and M.A. from the University of Wisconsin-Madison. In 1964, he earned an M.S.L from Columbia. He worked as a librarian in Performing Arts Research of the New York Pu ic Library from 1962-1970 and was an assistant professor and humanities librarian at Tren State College from 1970-1986.

Now writing fu time, Avi interacts with children in talks at schools about his writing.

Avi married Jc Gabriner, a weaver, in 1963 (divorced) and later married Coppelia Kahn, an English profe r. He has two children and a stepson.

Other Books Avi:
The Man W! Was Poe; Punch with Judy; The Barn; The Bird, the Frog, and the Light: A Fable; Blue Heron; Brig! Shadow; Captain Grey; City of Light/City of Dark: A Comic Book Novel; Devil's Race; Emily Uphc 's Revenge: A Massachusetts Adventure; Encounter at Easton; The Fighting Ground (Novel Units ides available)*; The History of Helpless Harry: To Which Is Added a Variety of Amusing and Enter ning Adventures; Man from the Sky; Night Journeys; No More Magic; A Place Called Ugly; Pop ; Romeo and Juliet, Together (and Alive) at Last; S.O.R. Losers; Smuggler's Island; Somethi Upstairs* (Novel Units guides available)*; Sometimes I Think I Hear My Name; Tom, Babette &*

Simon: Three Tales of Transformation; The True Confessions of Charlotte Doyle (Novel Units guides available); *"Who Was That Masked Man, Anyway?"; Windcatcher; Wolf Rider: A Tale of Terror*

Introductory Information and Activities

Initiating Activities:

1. Read aloud the two questions at the beginning of the book, perhaps repeating them twice with dramatic effect. Identify the questions. Talk especially about the second question. What might be included in a book with such a start?

2. This book is satire. What is it? Give some examples and then suggest what to look for in such writing.

3. The book is described as a documentary novel. What is that? *(It is a novel comprised of documents or portions of documents; no direct narrative is given.)* What do you predict?

4. Complete the Anticipation Guide found on page 5 of this guide.

5. Play the U.S. national anthem. When is it played? How do you react? Collect your ideas on a web.

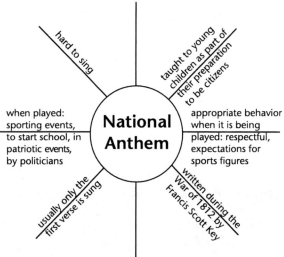

6. This book explores the interface of students, teachers, administration, community, media, and school board. What kind of documents do you expect that the author will use to tell the story?

7. Look carefully at the memo in the book on pages 1 and 2. What can you learn and infer about the Harrison School District and Joseph Palleni from the memo?

8. What do you know of the author Avi? What do you predict for a book written by him?

4

Anticipation Guide

Directions: Respond to each statement either agreeing, disagreeing, or undecided, before reading the book. The statements deal with some of the themes and issues in the book. After reading, return to this sheet to respond again and note any changes.

<u>Agree</u>	<u>Disagree</u>	<u>Undecided</u>			<u>Agree</u>	<u>Disagree</u>	<u>Undecided</u>
___	___	___	1.	It's a free country.	___	___	___
___	___	___	2.	Politics makes strange bedfellows.	___	___	___
___	___	___	3.	"Children and fools tell the truth."—Thomas Fuller	___	___	___
___	___	___	4.	"It takes two to speak the truth—one to speak, and another to hear."—H. D. Thoreau	___	___	___
___	___	___	5.	"Telling the truth to people who misunderstand you is generally promoting falsehood."—Anthony Hope Hawkins	___	___	___
___	___	___	6.	"A truth that's told with bad intent beats all the lies you can invent."—William Blake	___	___	___

Using Predictions

We all make predictions as we read—little guesses about what will happen next, how the conflict will be resolved, which details given by the author will be important to the plot, which details will help to fill in our sense of a character. Students should be encouraged to predict, to make sensible guesses. As students work on predictions, these discussion questions can be used to guide them: What are some of the ways to predict? What is the process of a sophisticated reader's thinking and predicting? What clues does an author give us to help us in making our predictions? Why are some predictions more likely than others?

A predicting chart is for students to record their predictions. As each subsequent chapter is discussed, you can review and correct previous predictions. This procedure serves to focus on predictions and to review the stories.

Use the facts and ideas the author gives.

Use your own knowledge.

Use new information that may cause you to change your mind.

Predictions:

_____

_____

_____

_____

Prediction Chart

What characters have we met so far?	What is the conflict in the story?	What are your predictions?	Why did you make those predictions?

Story Map

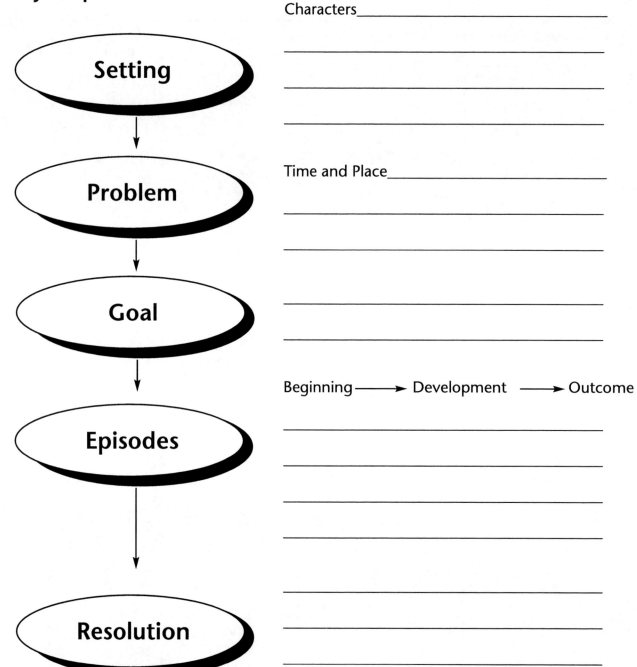

Setting

↓

Problem

↓

Goal

↓

Episodes

↓

Resolution

Characters_____

_____

_____

_____

Time and Place_____

_____

_____

_____

Beginning ——→ Development ——→ Outcome

_____

_____

_____

_____

_____

_____

_____

_____

Using Character Webs

Attribute Webs are simply a visual representation of a character from the novel. They provide a systematic way for the students to organize and recap the information they have about a particular character. Attribute webs may be used after reading the novel to recapitulate information about a particular character or completed gradually as information unfolds, done individually, or finished as a group project.

One type of character attribute web uses these divisions:

- How a character acts and feels. (How does the character feel in this picture? How would you feel if this happened to you? How do you think the character feels?)

- How a character looks. (Close your eyes and picture the character. Describe him to me.)

- Where a character lives. (Where and when does the character live?)

- How others feel about the character. (How does another specific character feel about our character?)

In group discussion about the student attribute webs and specific characters, the teacher can ask for backup proof from the novel. You can also include inferential thinking.

Attribute webs need not be confined to characters. They may also be used to organize information about a concept, object or place.

Attribute Web

The attribute web below is designed to help you gather clues the author provides about what a character is like. Fill in the blanks with words and phrases which tell how the character acts and looks, as well as what the character says and what others say about him or her.

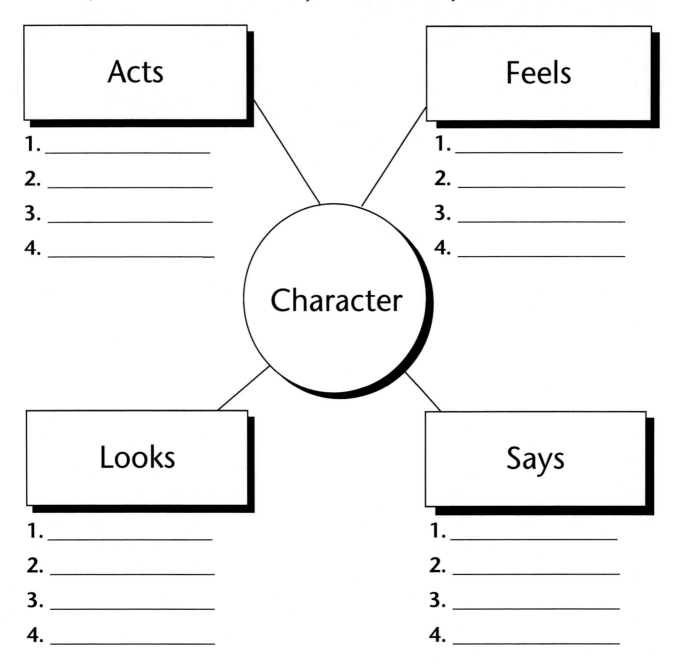

Attribute Web

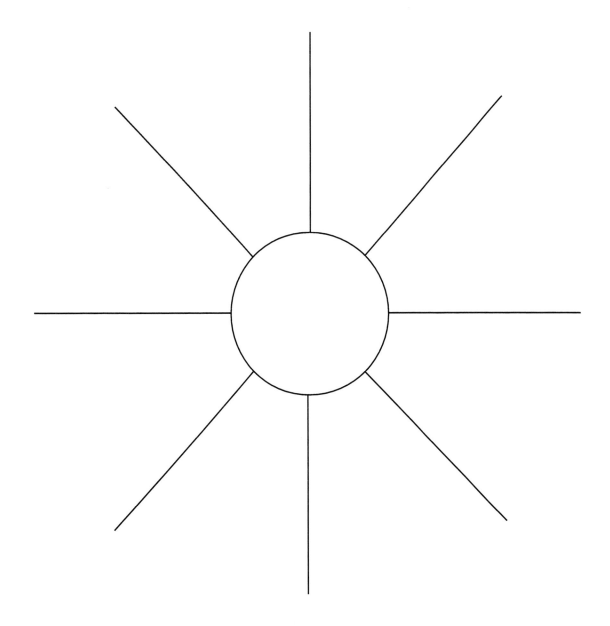

Chapter 1: "Tuesday, March 13"—Pages 3-6

Vocabulary:

steadfast 5   middling 5

Discussion Questions and Activities:

1. Who are the main characters of the book? From what viewpoint is the book written? *(Not clear; Philip Malloy and Margaret Narwin in their own words look to figure prominently.)*

2. Why are there incomplete sentences in the book? *(Philip's journal and Margaret's letters are informal writing. The author strives to make them seem authentic.)*

3. What is the setting of the story? *(a middle class high school in America, not particularly distinguished)*

4. What is the basic conflict which the author is setting up? *(Pages 4-5, Philip doesn't care for the dry traditional curriculum taught in Margaret Narwin's class. Narwin considers him a middling student with no particular desire to learn. Philip considers his English teacher "so uptight she must have been put together with super glue.")*

Supplementary Activities:

1. Start attribute webs for the main characters (See pages 10-11 of this guide.)

2. Look for a summary of *The Call of the Wild* by Jack London in the library. Ask the librarian for her opinion of the book.

Chapter 2: "Thursday, March 15"—Pages 7-10

Vocabulary:

carpe diem 7   assassinated 7   ramparts 8

Discussion Questions and Activities:

1. What kind of a teacher is Mr. Lunser? Compare him to Margaret Narwin. *(Lunser jokes around, with a humorous and slightly sarcastic comment for each part of the school opening activities. Narwin is traditional, follows rules to a T, and is respectful towards the administration.)*

2. What is Philip especially interested in during March? *(He has some minor concerns about term exams but mostly he's excited about trying out for the track team.)*

3. What are the primary concerns of the members of Philip's household? *(his mother—the health plan offered by her employer, his father—track)*

Supplementary Activities:
1. Get a copy of *Running* magazine. What can we learn about a character or friend or acquaintance from what they read? What magazines might you read? Conduct a class survey about the magazines read.

2. Keep track of the number of times that the words <u>truth</u> or <u>true</u> are used in the book. How does repetition increase their impact?

3. When have you heard the phrase "Carpe diem" before? How would you respond to such a comment by a teacher? Make a class list of things you'd do to "capture the day."

Chapter 3: "Friday, March 16"—Pages 11-14

Vocabulary:
facilitate 11

Discussion Questions and Activities:
1. What is the importance of the memo Philip receives from Dr. Joseph Palleni? *(His homeroom is being changed to Miss Narwin's.)* How do you expect that Philip feels about the news? *(not positive)*

2. Why does Philip call Allison Doresett? *(Ostensibly, he calls to check on the English book but probably he calls because he is interested in talking to her. He does talk about plans to try out for the track team.)*

Supplementary Activities:
(Students may answer in writing, orally, or with a drawing.)

1. How do opinions about books vary? Why do you think Allison and Philip in the book differ?

2. What kind of books do you like? Create a class list of alternatives to *The Call of the Wild.*

Chapter 4: "Monday, March 19"—Pages 15-16

Vocabulary:
symbolic 15   portrayal 15

Discussion Questions and Activities:
1. How does Philip answer his English exam question four? What is his attitude and manner? *(His answer is flippant and lacking in respect.)*

2. What is your opinion of Miss Narwin's comment on Philip's exam paper? *(Answers will vary.)*

3. **Prediction:** What will Philip's winter term grade be and how will he react?

Supplementary Activities:
1. Make a comparison of Philip and Miss Narwin. Create an illustration or make collages for each of them.

2. Start a listing of the reasons that Malloy and Narwin disagree.

Chapter 5: "Tuesday, March 20"—Pages 17-19

Vocabulary:
beneficiaries 18

Discussion Questions and Activities:
1. What do you learn of Margaret Narwin from her application for a grant? *(She is an experienced teacher and would like to get rejuvenated from a summer course. She is finding new students challenging and hard to understand. She has limited financial resources. She was the principal's English teacher when Dr. Doane was in high school.)*

2. What do you learn of the Harrison School District from the memo in Chapter 5? *(The heading indicates a professionalism and a desire to pass along a notion of the district's stated philosophy. The district has reduced and restricted money.)*

Supplementary Activities:
1. Ask your teachers or administrators about their English teachers. What is the nature of the best that they've encountered? Record on a web.

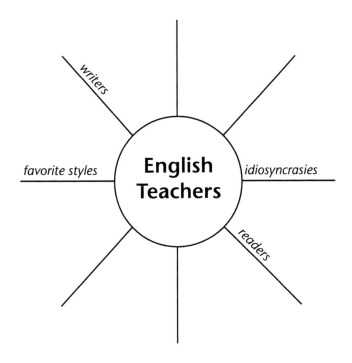

Chapter 6: "Wednesday, March 21"—Pages 20-21

Discussion Questions and Activities:

1. What do you learn of the school superintendent from his memo in Chapter 6? *(He has a doctorate, likes to address teachers as his colleagues, but is their boss. He is concerned about district finances. He is assertive.)*

2. What is *foreshadowing*? Look for a possible example in this chapter. *(Foreshadowing is the suggestion of events or issues to come later in a book. The suggestion of a controversial issue probably means that there will be such an item in the rest of the book.)*

Supplementary Activities:

1. Write an answer to Dr. Seymour from the head of the teachers' union.

2. The superintendent says, "Let me be blunt." (page 21) Cite examples of blunt writing in your experience. Choose one such incident to describe in a narrative piece of writing.

Chapter 7: "Friday, March 23"—Pages 22-23

Discussion Questions and Activities:
1. What wishes does Philip write into his diary entry for March 23? *(He wishes he hadn't thrown out Miss Narwin's comment on his English exam, and people would say what they mean.)*

2. Why do you think this chapter may be significant to the rest of the book? *(Answers will vary.)*

3. Find an example of hyperbole in the chapter. *(Page 23, "I'd give <u>anything</u> if I could be like him.")* What is hyperbole? *(extreme exaggeration)*

Supplementary Activities:
1. Collect some other examples of hyperbole; for example, "I'm starved," "I could eat a cow." Once a class collection is finished, choose one of the ideas to illustrate.

2. Describe an example from your own experience when a parent didn't say exactly what he or she meant.

Chapter 8: "Monday, March 26"—Pages 24-30

Vocabulary:

supportive 24	wholeheartedly 24	foreseen 25	allocated 25

Discussion Questions and Activities:
1. What is Dr. Doane's answer to Margaret Narwin's grant request? How is she informed? *(The answer is no and the request gets a formal memo answer with a lot of long words and a complimentary final paragraph.)*

2. How is March 26 similar for Margaret Narwin and for Philip Malloy? *(Both get bad news. Narwin is turned down for the grant and Philip finds out that he can't try out for track with a D grade.)*

3. How many times does Philip say, "I didn't know"? *(Pages 27-29, He says it three times. It's the theme of his conversation with Coach Earl Jamison.)*

4. What is Philip's attitude in English class and why does he feel the way he does? *(He is disappointed about not being able to try out for the track team and he acts surly and uninterested in class.)*

Supplementary Activities:

1. Phraseology: Translate each of the following phrases from the book, addressing what the speaker means and what might be implied from the words. How have you heard these same words used in your experiences?

	Meaning	Implication	Usage
"You can always count on me."			
"No one ever told me."			
"Sometimes you have to go along to get along."			
"Go with the flow."			
"A rule is a rule."			

Are these phrases clichés? What is a cliché?

2. How have outside forces added to the disagreements between Philip and Miss Narwin? Cite examples from the book.

Chapter 9: "Tuesday, March 27"—Pages 31-39

Vocabulary:

bickering 33   sprints 33   idiotic 36   outraged 36

Discussion Questions and Activities:

1. How is the Malloy parent conversation about grades typical of such conversations? *(They acknowledge the grades and then try to find out the reason. They each bring their own spin to the events, including differing views of grades and their own differing agendas.)*

2. What words on page 33 do the Malloys say that summarize their personal world views? *("Life isn't a sitcom." "The real world doesn't have a laugh track.")* How might you say the same idea in different words?

3. When his dad talks to Philip about grades, especially the English mark, and track team tryouts, how does Philip manage to hide the truth? *(He gives other reasons for not trying out for track, other than not being eligible. He skirts the real reasons for his poor English grade, focusing on the teacher not liking him. The reader knows that Miss Narwin holds no malice for him, but she wishes he were more serious about English class.)*

4. Explain Mr. Malloy's advice to Philip, "If God gives you a ticket, you better use it." *(Page 36, Answers will vary in their expression and explanation, but all will center around using your gifts.)*

5. How are respect, hurt, and truth revealed in Narwin's letter and Philip's diary? *(Narwin is hurt that she is denied the grant money in preference to a much younger teacher Kimberly Howard. She continues to feel that the rebuff is a lack of respect for her. Philip acknowledges that he skirted the truth in his answers to his dad.)*

6. How is the title of the book relevant in this chapter? *(Side issues color each character's reactions. <u>Nothing But The Truth</u> isn't the standard which they are using.)*

7. **Prediction:** How will homeroom be tomorrow for Philip? How will his attitudes and feelings be exhibited?

Supplementary Activities:
1. Reword maxims and adages which we all use in our interactions with others. Put these quotations from the book into your own words: "Life isn't a sitcom"; "The real world doesn't have a laugh track"; "If God gives you a ticket, you better use it"; "Go with the flow"; "You can always count on me."

2. Hit the bull's eye with the book's characters. Use the visual from page 20 of this guide to describe each main character.

3. Notice how each of the book's characters brings his or her own agendas to the interactions. Comment on personal agendas from your own experiences, as well as from the book and from other reading you have done.

Chapter 10: "Wednesday, March 28"—Pages 40-58

Vocabulary:

| frantic 48 | factually 52 | bedlam 55 | vigilant 55 |

Discussion Questions and Activities:
1. How does Philip's first day in Miss Narwin's homeroom work out? *(It is a bit chaotic with the new assignments. Philip hums along with the national anthem and Miss Narwin asks him to be quiet. He obeys.)*

2. How does Miss Narwin's style differ from Mr. Lunser's? *(Miss Narwin is more formal and takes the school rules more literally.)*

3. What does the faculty room conversation on pages 43-45 reveal about Margaret

Narwin? *(She is friendly toward Jacob Benison who is retiring this year. She is still irritated about not receiving the grant. She is disturbed by Philip's national anthem humming. She wants to make sure that she is in line with the rest of the faculty in terms of enforcing rules.)*

4. What do you think is Philip's real reason for humming during the national anthem in Miss Narwin's homeroom? Try to suggest several possibilities. *(patriotic, habit, wants to bug Narwin, hopes to be removed from the homeroom, irritable, revenge because of the bad English grade, wants to impress other students)*

5. On page 55, Philip writes in his diary, "Today was rotten." What happened to make him feel that way? *(He is assigned to Miss Narwin for homeroom, is asked to stop humming during the national anthem, irritates Narwin by smart remark/"joke" in English class, his lunch companion likes Narwin, Allison Doresett sits next to him on the bus but is put off by his irritable manner, and his parents ask him about the track team during dinner but he dodges the issue and tries to explain about the humming in homeroom.)*

6. Notice how the truth of the humming in homeroom incident changes slightly with retelling and exaggeration creeps in. Quote examples from the book. *(Page 44, Narwin describes the humming as very loud humming. Page 46, Philip talks about singing the national anthem to Todd Becker. Page 49, Narwin talks to Mr. Lunser. Page 53, Philip allows his parents to get a somewhat exaggerated version of the humming incident.)*

7. Why does Margaret Narwin need a *soothing*? What is a *soothing*? *(Page 55, She is unhappy with the new homeroom assignments and the general situation at school. She needs to be reassured and pampered a bit.)*

8. What is his father's advice to Philip? *(Page 58, "You stick up for your rights.")* How do you think that advice will affect the rest of the story?

Supplementary Activities:
1. Create a multi-frame cartoon/illustration to review the incidents in this chapter. (See page 21 of this guide.)

2. Review the action and story so far with a story map. (See page 8 of this guide.)

3. Suggest adverbs to describe the manner and emotional tone for each section of this chapter.

4. With a partner, agree on a one word reaction from different characters for these items/people: *The Call of the Wild*, Julius Caesar, Miss Narwin, Philip Malloy, morning announcements, homerooms, track, and correction by superiors/teachers.

Hit the Target with Characters

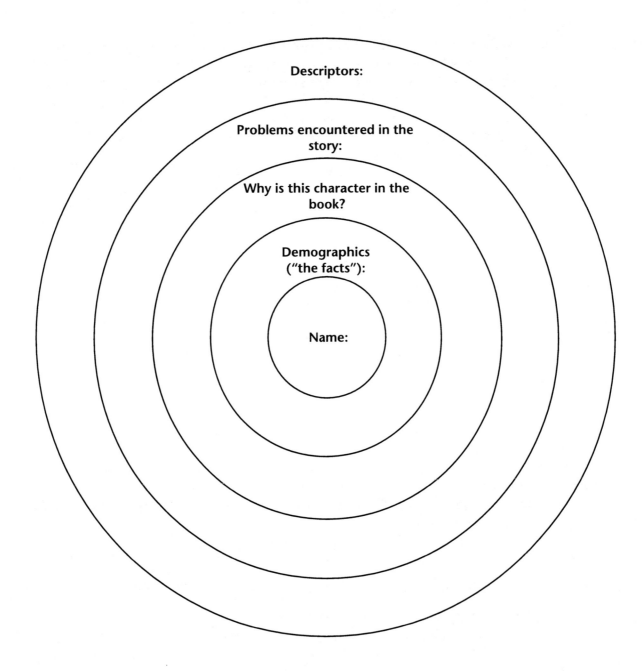

Descriptors:

Problems encountered in the story:

Why is this character in the book?

Demographics ("the facts"):

Name:

Comic Strips

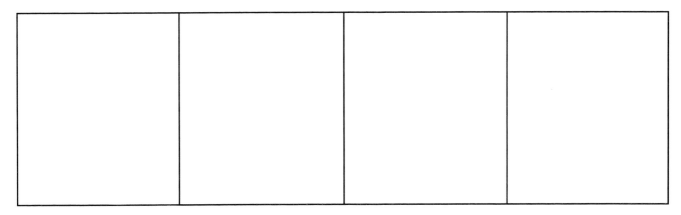

Some graphics to help:

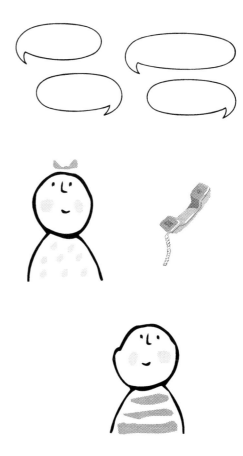

Chapter 11: "Thursday, March 29"—Pages 59-70

Vocabulary:

insolence 60   disobedient 63   infractions 63   botched 64

complexities 70

Discussion Questions and Activities:

1. How does the national anthem humming escalate in homeroom? *(Philip hums along with the tape of the national anthem and then doesn't stop when asked to by Miss Narwin, who then sends him to the assistant principal's office.)*

2. How does it go for Philip at Dr. Palleni's office? *(Pages 62-64, The assistant principal listens quickly to Philip's explanation and shows Philip the memo about morning announcements. [See page 1 of the book.] Palleni cuts the conversation short and doesn't act on Philip's request for a change in homeroom, sending Philip on his way with, "Have a nice day.")*

3. How might Palleni's statement "We're into solving problems, not making them" be foreshadowing? *(Page 61, Answers will vary.)*

4. Why is the conversation between Mr. Malloy and his boss, Mr. Dexter, included in the book? *(to help the reader understand Mr. Malloy's viewpoint and feelings, to draw a parallel to Philip's situation)*

5. Compare the 6:10 and 7:10 entries in the book. *(Pages 67-69, When Mrs. Malloy hears about her husband's disagreement at work, she admonishes him to stand up for himself. Likewise, Mr. Malloy admonishes Philip to stand up for himself in his dealings about the national anthem humming.)*

6. Compare the 9:45 and 11:05 entries in the book. *(Pages 69-70, Peg Narwin is pleased that her principal is different and announces that she's lucky. Philip writes that his parents are different and he's lucky.)*

7. How might the lucky and standing up for yourself statements be ironic as the story unfolds? *(Page 70, The entire story hasn't been told yet but the repetition of the statements creates emphasis and makes the reader wonder about whether the opposite situation might be going to happen.)*

Supplementary Activities:

1. Answer Philip Malloy's question on page 63, "Is a memo a rule?" First, discuss with classmates, parents, and teachers. Then write a short paragraph answer, explaining your reasoning.

2. What do you think of Dr. Palleni's dismissal to Philip after their talk? How does his answer tell you about his understanding of Philip?

3. Act out the conversations in this chapter. Try to reveal the real natures.

4. How authentic is the book? Does Avi give you conversations that really might have taken place? Give reasons for your answers and do refer to the book.

Chapter 12: "Friday, March 30"—Pages 71-103

Vocabulary:

suspension 74	bygones 77	infraction 83	obscure 89
disruptive 94	arbitrary 96	condone 100	

Discussion Questions and Activities:
1. How does Philip react in homeroom after getting support from his parents? *(He hums along with the recording of the national anthem and refuses to stop when requested. He tells his teacher that he has the right to do it and adds that she's being disrespectful and he's being patriotic. She sends him to the principal's office.)*

2. How does Dr. Palleni react to seeing Philip twice in a week for disciplinary matters? *(He offers Philip the option to apologize to Miss Narwin as an alternative to a two-day suspension. Philip refuses and so Mrs. Malloy is summoned to school to take Philip home.)*

3. Should Philip have apologized? What would you have done? *(Answers will vary.)*

4. How are the characters in the book at listening to each other? Do they really hear and understand what is being said to them? Give examples from the book to explain and support your answer. *(Dr. Palleni doesn't hear that Philip really wants out of Narwin's class. Mr. Malloy is preoccupied with his job situation. Both Malloy parents don't recognize that the low grade in English and Philip's exclusion from track tryouts are a large part of their son's actions. Miss Narwin doesn't recognize the importance of the English grade in Philip's life.)*

5. Who is Ted Griffen and how does he figure in the plot of the story? *(a neighbor of the Malloys who is running for the school board)*

6. Notice the dashes on page 84. What do they indicate? *(Dr. Palleni cuts off Mrs. Malloy when she talks to him.)*

7. What is the flavor of the memos Dr. Palleni sends about the suspension? *(The focus is on the disrespect issue and breaking of a rule. There is no mention of patriotism or the national anthem.)*

8. Philip writes in his diary, "It really hit the fan today." *(page 103)* What is his message? *(The two-day suspension put him into trouble at school and talking to the newspaper reporter and Ted Griffen added fuel to the flames.)*

9. Why doesn't Philip feel so great at the end of the day? *(He understands that the whole humming incident during the national anthem is stupid. A really big deal is being made of it and all Philip wanted was to be able to try out for track.)*

10. How will the reporter change the course of the events of the story? Make some predictions.

Supplementary Activities:
1. Discussion: Was Philip right? How could Dr. Palleni have been more helpful? Why is Mr. Malloy pushing the matter to another level?

2. Advice Columnist: If the people involved in the controversy had written to you, what advice would you give?

3. How do parents react when the school calls them?

Chapter 13: "Saturday, March 31"—Pages 104-117

Vocabulary:
disturbance 113

Discussion Questions and Activities:
1. How would you title this chapter if the author asked you? *(Encourage a variety of answers: "Politics," "The Media Gets Into It," "The Power of the Phone.")*

2. How does Jennifer Stewart go about checking her facts before writing an article for the newspaper? *(She starts at the top with the superintendent of schools and then moves down.)*

3. How do each of the parties react when asked about the suspension by Jennifer Stewart? *(superintendent—matter-of-fact, cordial; principal—cordial, uninformed; assistant principal—irritated, uncommunicative; teacher—cordial, but unwilling to give a lot of detail)*

4. **Prediction:** Will Philip talk to Miss Narwin? How will she react? What will be the outcome?

Supplementary Activities:
1. Notice how the story changes and the spin on it changes with each phone call. Play a round of the old game *Telephone.* (The first person whispers a message to another person who repeats it to the next player and so on down the line. The message invariably changes in the transmission.) Why does the story in this book also seem to change as it goes from person to person? What principles for communication might you notice herein?

2. Write a news article that Jennifer Stewart might write about the incident. What headline might you use?

3. Imagine the headlines which would appear for an article about "the incident" if the article were written from these different points of view—Dr. Doane, Miss Narwin, Dr. Palleni, the track coach.

Chapter 14: "Sunday, April 1"—Pages 118-126

Discussion Questions and Activities:
1. What is the tone of the article about Philip in the *Manchester Record?* Look carefully for loaded words and other ways that the news writer has slanted the piece. *(It is favorable toward Philip, has repeated use of the word patriotism, and most of the article focuses on Philip and his parents. The final paragraph mentions the upcoming school referendum.)*

2. Look for possible foreshadowing in this chapter. *(Page 121, "No one reads about schools." Page 124, "Just tell people the truth. Put your faith in that." Page 124, "It will pass.")* How might foreshadowing be used in an ironic tale? *(The opposite might happen.)*

3. How does Ted Griffen maneuver in this chapter? *(He uses the national anthem suspension in his political speeches—condemning what happened in the school and promising to do better.)*

4. Why is the date especially significant? *(It is April Fool's Day and the real foolishness is just getting started.)*

Supplementary Activities:
1. Could this happen in your school? Why or why not? Talk it over with your teacher and principal.

2. What are the rules at your school for sports eligibility?

3. Look at your local newspaper for news of the schools. How is your school system covered in the press? Collect school press for the time you finish reading the book. Compare your coverage to that in the book.

Chapter 15: "Monday, April 2"—Pages 127-167

Vocabulary:

balmy 130	squelches 139	commotion 140	provocative 141
infractions 142	indicative 155	animosity 155	suppression 156
assault 157	elemental 163		

Discussion Questions and Activities:
1. What is the AAP Wire Service? *(It is the American Affiliated Press Wire Service, a wire service which distributes various local news stories.)* How does Philip's situation change when the story is picked up by the AAP? *(There is national attention to the matter, including a call-in talk show.)*

2. Who is Jake Barlow? *(a talk show entertainer who tells his listeners about Philip's suspension)*

3. Why is it ironic that Jake Barlow announces to his listeners that he's telling them the whole story (pages 128-129) about Philip Malloy? *(The AAP news wire is a reprint of the Manchester article which was slanted in favor of Philip.)*

4. Why is Gloria Harland calling Dr. Seymour at 8:07 A.M.? *(She alerts the superintendent to the comments by Ted Griffen about the national anthem matter.)* How does Dr. Seymour react? *(He is upset, especially with a school budget vote coming up soon. He promises to get back to Mrs. Harland with details about the incident.)*

5. How does Jake Barlow turn up the heat on the national anthem discussion? *(He makes it clear that he is opposed to the school and the teacher and in favor of Philip. He refers to Philip as an "American patriot." Later, page 139, he asks his listeners to write to the school and Margaret Narwin with their opinions. He is supportive of Philip and attacks a listener who tries to support the teacher and suggests that there is more to the story.)*

6. What is Dr. Seymour's message in his 8:30 A.M. call to Dr. Doane? *(He tells her about Ted Griffen's use of the national anthem incident in his school board campaigning. He wants a short memo of explanation that he can read out about the incident ASAP.)*

7. Explain Seymour's statement, "It's what people are saying that's important."
(Page 133, The truth of the situation is less important than what people think happened. Perception and appearances are important, especially with public opinion.)

8. Reread the conversation between Doane, Narwin, and Palleni on pages 140-142. Is it authentic-sounding? Why do they "need to tell the same story"? *(The three professionals want to be ready to answer questions about the incident. They want to avoid criticism.)*

9. Compare the three drafts of memos about the national anthem incident. Why do they differ? What is happening to the truth? How is the impression changing?

Pages 143-144—Memo: Philip's humming is described as loud, raucous singing. Detail and rationale for the suspension are included. Palleni is the writer of this draft.

Pages 154-156—Memo Rewritten by Dr. Doane: The memo is longer. Philip's humming is still described as loud, raucous singing but also to draw attention to himself. A comment is added that there has been no history of disturbance during the national anthem. Also included are a report of discussion with other students about the incident, a suggestion of personal animosity between Narwin and Malloy, a discussion of Philip's English work and grade with Miss Narwin, and an emphasis of respect toward the national anthem.

Pages 158-160—Memo Written by Dr. Seymour: The memo is longer yet. Morning exercises in all Harrison schools are described. The humming is now loud, raucous, disrespectful, drawing attention to himself and away from the words. There are strong indications of personal animosity between Philip and Miss Narwin. Also included is the indication that Philip was given the opportunity to dispute the facts of the incident. Students confirm these facts. He chose the suspension option himself.

10. What significant details do Ken Barchet, Cynthia Gambia, and Allison Doresett give to Dr. Doane about the national anthem incident? How does she use these details in her memo? *(Barchet is hesitant, unsure about the details and isn't sure if Philip had been singing but not loudly. He doesn't think the class noticed much about the noise. Cynthia says she wasn't paying much attention, except that Philip hummed and it wasn't loud but that he was being sort of rude. Allison Doresett adds that Philip doesn't like Miss Narwin and he sometimes made remarks that were jokes or funny. She thinks Philip was trying to get at Miss Narwin. Philip had been moody lately. She adds that she likes Miss Narwin. Doane uses the details that are negative toward Philip in her memo.)*

© Novel Units, Inc.   All rights reserved

27

11. How has the whole thing gotten out of hand? *(The telegrams of support and criticism are riling everyone up. Peg Narwin gets a call from her sister in Florida who reads her an account in the Florida paper about the incident. She's upset.)*

12. Predict how Miss Narwin will react to Philip's request for extra work to improve his grade and be able to get on the track team.

Supplementary Activities:
1. Compose a telegram you'd send to either Philip or Miss Narwin.

2. What questions should Jake Barlow ask about the national anthem incident in the interest of responsible journalism?

3. Compose a memo that tells the truth about the incident.

Chapter 16: "Tuesday, April 3"—Pages 168-200

Vocabulary:

dismayed 169	outraged 170	incredible 175	misconstrue 177
marrow 186	tenure 187	expedite 194	sabbatical 194
equitable 198	fiscally 198	prudent 198	

Discussion Questions and Activities:
1. Why does Dr. Seymour describe the mood among the people as outraged? *(That is how they feel. The feelings have been flamed by Ted Griffen's politicking and the media reports about their school.)*

2. How does Dr. Seymour react? *(Pages 171-172, He says that he doesn't care about the board but the budget vote does worry him. He says, "Whatever it takes." He plans to do whatever he can to get a positive vote on the school budget.)*

3. How many telegrams came to Miss Narwin and the school? *(almost two hundred)*

4. Miss Narwin says she pleaded with Joe not to suspend Philip. *(page 176)* Is it *nothing but the truth? (No. She mildly disagreed with Dr. Palleni, but it was hardly pleading.)*

5. How is the school policy changed about the national anthem? *(An official statement indicates that there is no rule that prohibits a student from singing along with the national anthem recording if he/she so desires.)*

6. How does the plot really take a change in this chapter? *(Philip tries to talk to Miss Narwin about extra work but she stops him cold because he has been changed to another teacher. Miss Narwin is asked to take the rest of the semester off and funds are found for her to take the summer course she had requested. The superintendent meets with Ted Griffen who comes out in support of the school budget.)*

7. Find these phrases in the chapter and explain what they mean.

   "...my job is to make sure these kids get educated. Whatever it takes." (page 172)

   "You can't blame yourself..." (page 176)

   "...people will misconstrue." (page 177)

   "You've got a problem there." (page 187)

   "...a rule is a rule." (page 192)

8. How do Philip and Miss Narwin seem similar at the end of the chapter? *(Both don't know what they are going to do.)*

9. Why does the superintendent turn on Miss Narwin? *(Answers vary.)*

10. Why does the coach turn on Philip? *(Answers vary.)*

11. **Prediction:** How will the novel end?

Supplementary Activities:
   1. How is this chapter a turning point in the book? What is a turning point?

   2. Suggest a title for this chapter.

   3. What might Philip say to the whole school if he had the chance? What might Miss Narwin say in similar circumstances?

   4. What other documentary pieces of information might the author have added in this novel?

Chapter 17: "Wednesday, April 4"—Pages 201-207

Vocabulary:
   desperately 206   assaulted 206

Discussion Questions and Activities:
1. How do Narwin and Malloy react in similar fashion in this chapter? *(Both decide not to go to school.)*

2. How does Miss Narwin describe her frame of mind to Robert Duval? *(Page 206, She's been "assaulted.")* Is she justified? *(Answers will vary.)*

Supplementary Activities:
1. Write Mr. Duval's news article.

2. Who are the good guys and bad guys in this story? Defend your answers with evidence from the story.

Chapter 18: "Friday, April 6"—Pages 208-210

Vocabulary:
candid 209

Discussion Questions and Activities:
1. What do you learn from the *Manchester Record* school election returns? *(The budget is defeated and Ted Griffen is elected to the school board. Twenty-two percent of the eligible voters cast ballots.)*

2. Why isn't Margaret Narwin's story told? *(Breaking news keeps the piece out of the St. Louis paper and the interest in the national anthem incident seems to have waned.)*

3. What will Margaret Narwin do? *(She will spend the rest of the term with her sister in Florida. Answers will vary about her future prospects.)*

Supplementary Activities:
1. What is the mood and tone of Chapter 18? How did you feel reading it? Explain your answer in a short paragraph.

2. How do newspapers decide what to print? Talk to a local newspaper person to get an answer.

Chapter 19: "Monday, April 9"—Pages 211-212

Discussion Questions and Activities:
1. What happens to Philip at the book's end? *(He goes to Washington Academy.)*

2. What are the final ironies of the book? *(The new school doesn't have a track team and Philip admits that he doesn't know the words to the national anthem.)*

Culminating Activities

1. Write Philip's honest diary entry after a week at Washington Academy.

2. Compose letters from Margaret Narwin to Philip Malloy, Gertrude Doane, and Jacob Benison. (See page 43 of the book.)

3. If you were on the school advisory board, what advice would you give to the principal of Harrison High School?

4. Cause-and-Effect: What caused the national anthem incident? Complete the Cause-and-Effect chart on page 34 of this guide.

5. How did the players in the story make decisions? Use the Decision-Making Chart on page 33 of this guide to summarize your thoughts.

6. Return to the Anticipation Guide. Have your ideas changed and why?

7. Create a mind map to show the various points of view that are exposed and revealed in the book. Sort out the core truth of the story and discuss it in a short paragraph.

8. How did the two main characters change from the beginning of the book to the end?

Vocabulary Activities

1. Sort out the words identified in the various chapters into categories. For example, descriptions, action, educational words, teenage expressions.

2. Display the words on a word wall or other chart in the classroom. Students work in pairs, learning the words and then accepting the challenge to get a partner to say a specified number of the words in a specified amount of time. The challenger gives definitions or other helps. (Obviously, saying the word itself would be unacceptable.)

3. Keep track of how many times in a day you can use the words. The classroom's highest user gets a reward. (possibly extra credit)

4. Choose five or six of the words to investigate etymologically. That is, look up where the words came from, what their roots are.

5. Start a list of prefixes and suffixes which you find in the identified vocabulary words.

6. Act out some of the words, dramatically or in rap.

7. Use one of these prompts to recall the words. Attach a word for each of the letters.

S	I	D
A	R	O
T	O	C
I	N	U
R	Y	M
E		E
		N
		T
		A
		R
		Y

Making Decisions

Problem: State the character's problem in the book.

Solutions: Choose three to seven possible solutions.

      (a) State each choice in a short sentence.

      (b) Design three to five "criteria" (questions you can ask to measure how good a particular choice may be)

      (c) Rate the criteria for each solution: 1=yes 2=maybe 3=no

SOLUTIONS ↓	CRITERIA				
1.					
2.					
3.					
4.					
5.					
6.					
7.					

Cause-Effect

Directions: To plot cause and effect in a story, first list the sequence of events. Then mark causes with a C and effects with an E. Sometimes in a chain of events, one item may be both a cause and an effect. Draw arrows from cause statements to the appropriate effects.

Events in the story:

1.

2.

3.

4.

5.

6.

7.

8.

9.

10.

Another way to map cause and effect is to look for an effect and then backtrack to the single or multiple causes.

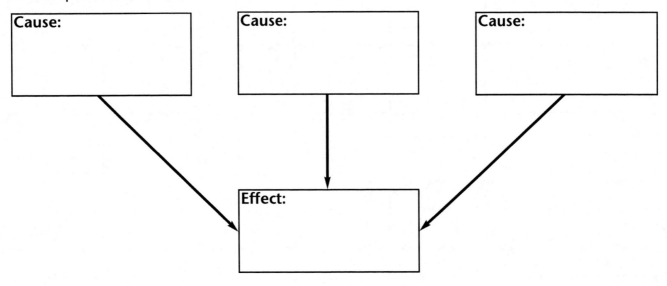

Assessment for *Nothing But The Truth*

Overview:

Assessment is an on-going process, more than a single test. The following ten items can be completed during the novel study. Student and teacher can check off items as finished. Points may be added to indicate the level of understanding.

STUDENT   **TEACHER**

_____   _____   1. Define these terms associated with the book: satire, irony, and documentary fiction.

_____   _____   2. Keep a predicting chart while reading the book.

_____   _____   3. Present three character webs for selected book characters.

_____   _____   4. Summarize five of the book's characters with three significant words.

_____   _____   5. Speculate how Philip and Miss Narwin will fare in the year following the end of the book.

_____   _____   6. Create an additional documentary piece of evidence which might have been included in the book. Use your creativity but do remain true to the sense of the book.

_____   _____   7. Explain what the book's title means in a short paragraph.

_____   _____   8. Choose three vocabulary activities to complete.

_____   _____   9. Summarize the plot with a comprehensive story map, a narrative explanation, or a short reader's theater presentation.

_____   _____   10. Give the book three, four, or five thumbs up to indicate your evaluation of the book. Defend your rating in a short paragraph.

Notes